GET IN
—IF YOU WANT TO—
LIVE

FOR KATE & THEO

The following stories have previously appeared in other publications: Recently I Passed A Kidney Stone That Looks Like A Shark's Tooth (*McSweeney's*), The Monroe Family Bed Wishes To Die (*McSweeney's*), Yes, I Totally Spaced Telling You About That Lair In My Basement (*Opium*), Javier (*Paper Darts Magazine*), I Only Have Sex With Ladies Named Jean (*The Tangential*), A Toast To Randy, The Oldest Son Of My Secret Family (*McSweeney's*), I Am So Sorry That My Homing Device Was Chafing Your Ankle (*Opium*), My Codpiece Smells Like Soup (*McSweeney's*), James, I Cannot Even Begin To Imagine Who Threw A Bag Of Shit Into Your Dishwasher (*McSweeney's*), Sorry, But I Just Can't Marry A Woman That Doesn't Look Hot On The Jumbotron (*Yankee Pot Roast*), My Best Friend Joe Looks Like Handel And I Look Like Beethoven (*Vita.mn*), The Future (*Opium*), Get In If You Want To Live (*METRO*).

TABLE OF CONTENTS

RECENTLY I PASSED A KIDNEY STONE THAT LOOKS LIKE A SHARK'S TOOTH

ILLUSTRATED BY ANDRES GUZMAN

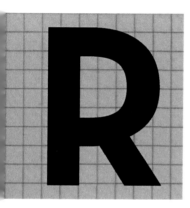

ecently I passed a kidney stone that looks like a shark's tooth. I made it into a necklace and now I wear it everywhere I go. It is a very intriguing piece of jewelry. People are constantly asking me questions about it.

"That looks incredible," they say. "Where did you get it?"

"It shot out of my dick," I tell them.

Sometimes the kidney stones I pass look like cultured pearls. Once I collected a week's worth and made a necklace for my girlfriend Trisha.

I give Trisha lots of jewelry. On Valentine's Day or on Christmas, she'll always get a small box with something awesome in it that shot out of my penis.

Sometimes Trisha wonders where I get the money for all this jewelry. On her last birthday I gave her a pair of earrings. After she opened them, she put them up to her nose.

"These are absolutely lovely," she said, "but for some reason they smell like asparagus."

When I drink a lot of Mountain Dew my kidney stones look like jade and when I drink red wine they look like rubies. When I eat a lot of Skittles they look like they should—an amazing fucking rainbow. I want to ask Trisha to marry me, but I haven't figured out what I can eat or drink to make me shoot out a diamond. I drank Sprite for a month straight, but that didn't work. I want to have a diamond ring for the proposal and I'm gonna wait until my dick cooperates. I guess I'm old fashioned that way.

A couple of days ago, I rented a kiosk at the mall to sell some of the jewelry I've been producing lately. Things are going great. Sometimes people buy so much of my inventory that I have to go to the bathroom and make more.

I stand at the urinal and my piss goes ping, ping, ping against the ceramic. It's a very emotional experience and sometimes someone will walk into the bathroom while I'm crying and scooping the jewels out of the urinal.

"Why the fuck won't my cock shoot out diamonds?" I yell at them.

I keep asking everyone that comes into the bathroom that question, but so far nobody knows the answer.

MY KIDNAPPER GIVES A REALLY GOOD BACKRUB

ILLUSTRATED BY RUBEN IRELAND

My kidnapper, Randall, gives a really good backrub. He's got these long fingers that can really get into that knot in my shoulder. He gives a way better backrub than my last kidnapper, Ted.

"You should think about massage school," I tell Randall. "After you are done kidnapping me and after we get married, I mean."

Randall takes a pull on his bottle of whiskey. He tells me that wasn't a backrub, that he was just pinching my shoulder blade to immobilize me as he moved me back to my cage. I've only known him three hours, but I can tell he's just being modest. He's the exact opposite of that jackass Ted, who would not shut up about himself.

"I know what a good backrub feels like," I tell Randall. "And that was an awesome one."

Randall eats dinner with me in the tiny room he built below his basement. He tells me that this is as fast as he's ever seen someone get Stockholm Syndrome. I tell him he's never met my older sister, Janine. The first time Janine got kidnapped she fell in love with her kidnapper in ten minutes.

"That's a lot to live up to," I say. "That's still a California record."

Randall's also a really great cook. Tonight there's soup from a can, but I can tell it was prepared with a lot of affection.

"Maybe you should become a chef," I tell Randall as he picks his teeth with his switchblade. "Maybe after this is over then maybe kidnapping could just become your hobby."

Randall takes the coffee can that I pee in and dumps it out in the corner. I can't believe how gentle he's been with me since he cut off my pinky and sent it to my father. It's all I can do from kissing him all over his beardy face.

"Your dad better pay up, Blondie," Randall says as he turns off the light and leaves me in the dark to love him. "He better fucking pay up soon or you are one dead bitch."

I know I shouldn't get too excited, but I really like how quick this relationship is moving. That dummy Ted and I never had nicknames for each other, but Randall and I already do. Randall either calls me "Bitch" or "Blondie" or he simplifies everything and calls me "Blond Bitch." I usually call him "Honey" or "Randy."

A couple of hours later, I hear Randall upstairs on the phone. The conversation sounds heated. You don't have to tell me how hard it is to deal with my father. He makes me so tired sometimes. He's all like "we have that security detail for a reason, stop trying to ditch them" and "that's the third time you've been kidnapped this year, are you trying to make it happen?" And then once I get kidnapped he's all screamy with the kidnappers saying things like, "Gimme back my daughter or I'm going to track your ass down and cut your head off." It's really embarrassing and it makes me want to crawl into a hole deeper than that earthen pit Ted kept me in.

I fall asleep and dream of the life Randall and I will have with each other, but then I wake when I hear the men yelling upstairs. I hear Randall yelling that they're not going to take him alive. Then I hear gunshots. I wait for Randall to come downstairs to get me so we can hold each other and die some lovely intertwined death, but instead of him walking down the stairs, it's my father and one of the FBI guys that I know, Agent Rizzotti. Rizzotti helps me out of my cage and wraps me in a blanket. My father holds out his arms for a hug, but I walk right past him up the stairs and into the kitchen and I step over Randall's dead body and walk outside. I do not get into my father's car though, even when he yells at me. I just keep walking. I walk straight toward the highway and I hold out my thumb and wait for someone else new and exciting to drive by and abduct me so we can fall madly in love.

LOOTING

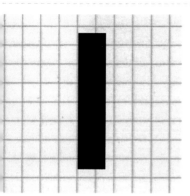came home from looting and found my neighbor Albert reclining in the Barcalounger that I'd looted the day before. He was drinking some of my looted beer from my stolen mini fridge and eating some peanut brittle that my mother had sent me for my birthday.

"Anything good left on those fine streets of ours?" he asked.

I looked out the window. There were still fires nearby, but they were smaller ones than the last few nights. They looked like they had been set mostly for warmth or grilling kebabs.

"It's getting pretty picked over by now," I told him.

I unzipped my suitcase and unloaded today's take. I'd spent most of my time in a RadioShack, but I'd scored all of the good stuff from the basement of this Polynesian restaurant. A bunch of these ceramic cups that looked like Easter Island statues.

"Jolene's leaving me," Albert said.

Jolene leaving Albert was not news. Last night, after I lugged that recliner inside my house, I'd found his wife, Jolene, naked in my bed. I did not know how these two kept on getting in here. What I needed to loot most of all was a new fucking deadbolt lock.

"I thought you might be interested in some fun," Jolene said.

Jolene was older than me, but she did not look it. She had not lived the hard life of looting like I had, with all the charred buildings and the angry people with the aluminum baseball bats. She curled her foot and put it on my thigh.

"I have a very strong moral code," I said.

"What the hell is that supposed to mean?" she asked.

"It means I'll steal anything except other people's women," I told her.

There were sirens now and their sound was getting closer with each hour. Both Albert and I agreed that their noise was progress. That in a couple of days there would be bulldozers and then a couple of days after that, the owners of the sub shops and shoe stores would go over to the banner shop and buy some sort of banner with an exclamation point telling the world that they were still here and that they were not going anywhere else.

"What are you going to do about Jolene?" I asked Albert.

"Beg her to come back," he said. "Then treat her like she thought she deserved."

I did not know what to say to that so I went over to the kitchen and poured him a glass of bourbon. I handed it to him and watched as he swirled it around in the glass, put his nose up to it, and took a whiff.

I could tell by the expression on his face that he understood that this bourbon was something special, that this was the good stuff, the expensive kind from the fancy glass bottle, the stuff that I'd actually gone out to a real store and bought.

I AM COMMITTED TO GETTING YOU YOUR HEROIN AT THE PEAK OF ITS FRESHNESS

ILLUSTRATED BY CARLEYRAE WEBER

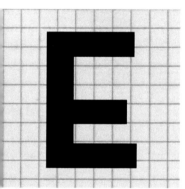

Each morning, I get up at 5:00 a.m. to go down to the docks. Why do I get up at this ungodly hour? Sometimes it is because I've been binging on whores with the shades drawn and I have forgotten if it is actually morning or night, but sometimes it is because I'm a consummate businessman who is 100 percent committed to making sure you, my customer, get really fresh heroin.

Sometimes I am driven by failure and sometimes I am driven by my driver, Carl. Sometimes when Carl picks me up in the morning there are bagels, but sometimes he brings donuts. Sometimes I am not in the mood for any breakfast at all and I say to Carl, "Let's go visit that guy over in the Bronx," and then we drive over there and Carl holds the man down while I electrocute him in the nuts.

Every morning when I am done I go back to my place to stack my money in different configurations (mostly pyramids and rhombuses) and I sit on a chair that is made entirely of gold and rubies. This chair is not very comfortable, but it was a present from my mother so I have to use it. I told my mother I wanted a throne with really good lumbar support and chafeless rubies, but she did not listen. No one would ever call this chair a throne unless they were totally cruel to me or unless I was pushing their head into a toilet until they called it that.

I work six days a week, making sure that my product arrives to you as quickly as humanly possible. I usually take Sundays off to drive upstate and search for truffles with my potbelly pig, Paco, but sometimes I will hit the estate sales or kill one of my competitors with a rusty machete that is a priceless family heirloom.

Sometimes I ask myself why I make such large sacrifices for you, my customer. But then I see you, leaning up against a burned out building, wearing your underwear outside your pants, and I know why I do what I do.

Sure, I know that sometimes you are ungrateful for my hard work, but I do not let it bother me. When I see you on the street, you ask me for the freshest heroin, and instead of giving you any sometimes I kill you with my machete and let Paco eat your eyes. Sometimes though, when I am having a really good day, I reach into my leather truffle bag and hand you a couple of truffles.

"Are these 'shrooms?" you yell as I walk back to my jewel-encrusted limo. "Will these get me high?"

I walk away without answering you, because guess what?

Tomorrow this shit starts all over again.

THE MONROE FAMILY BED WISHES TO DIE

ILLUSTRATED BY MEGAN FRAUENHOFFER

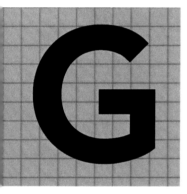

Good Evening, Tom and Connie, it's your family bed. I know this isn't very nice of me given your stance on euthanasia and Tom's chronic back problems, but since tonight one of your children spilled some rubbing alcohol on me and my tongue is loosened up, I'm going to take this opportunity to say what needs to be said. Here goes—I WANT TO DIE.

Please, before either of you speak, I want to tell you that this was not a decision entered into lightly. After a period of long and thoughtful soul-searching under the constant and crushing weight of your family's pear-shaped bodies, I have decided that I would like to end my life. I hope you will respect my wishes and not attempt to talk me out of it.

As you may have guessed, Tom and Connie, the final straw was the baby. Sure, the little tyke is adorable, he's your pride and joy, but unfortunately, he keeps pissing on me. I can put up with a lot—the eerily silent coitus that you two continue to engage in when you think your children are asleep, the corn-fed girth of a Midwestern family of six and a gassy golden retriever—but what kind of bed would I be if I just kept letting myself be pissed on night after night?

If the new baby was the extent of my burden, I might be able to stick it out. But there are other things that make me want to depart this earth. Tom, I know that you are between jobs and I understand that church law will not allow Connie to work. Those things said, could you two scrimp a bit in some area other than sheets? This last pair you put on me had a thread count of like eight. I swear to god they were made of yarn. I hope both of you can remember this after I am gone: sheets are a mattress's shirt. Do you know anyone who wears a motherfucking YARN shirt? Actually, you probably do.

Honestly, I've reached the point where I don't really care how it happens. Shove me out a frat window, cut me into tiny bits with a miter saw, set me on fire during a riot. Sadly this is where I have arrived—as long as I am put out of my misery by noon tomorrow, it does not really matter how I go.

I can see you shaking your heads, I can hear you saying that you can't, you couldn't, you won't. Listen, Tom and Connie—I didn't want to have to pull this card, but I'd like you to know that I will take measures to make sure my wish is fulfilled. What measures? I'd rather not have to spell it out for you, but let's just say that it starts with an "s" and ends with "uffication." Is that enough of a hint?

Anyway, let's push those unpleasant thoughts aside for now though, shall we? I know that it won't come to any of that. You are sensible, mattress-fearing people, and I know in my heart of hearts that you will heed this, my final request.

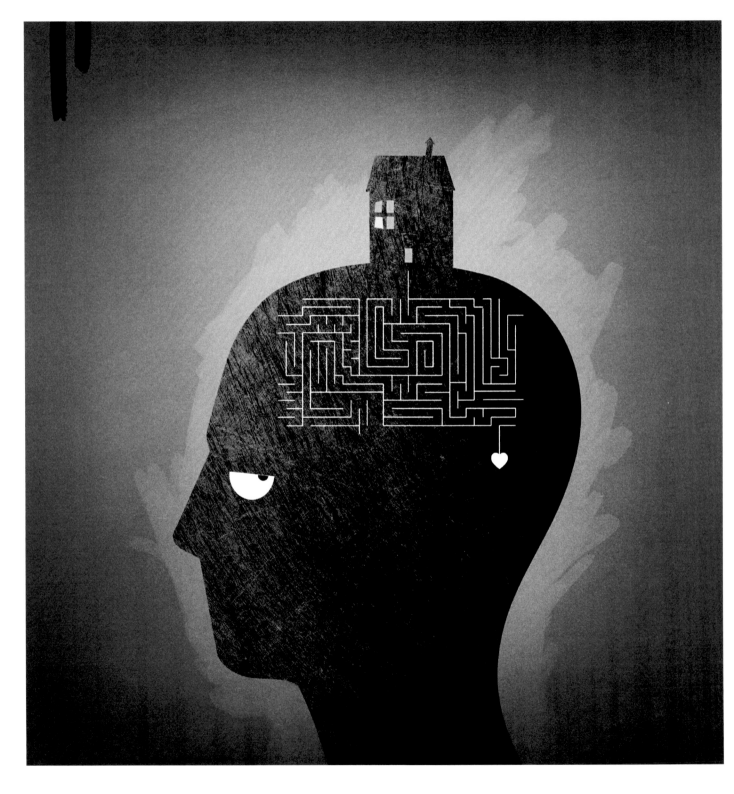

YES, I TOTALLY SPACED TELLING YOU ABOUT THAT LAIR IN MY BASEMENT

ILLUSTRATED BY AINARA DEL VALLE

So I have a "lair." So what? I can call it "the basement" if that makes you more comfortable. I can call it whatever you want. How about "John's Workshop?" Would that work? Because we are in a committed, loving relationship, I am willing to give a little here. I mean, I am not all that concerned about selling the naming rights anymore. I was for a while, but not now. I've come to accept the fact that the Internet boom is over and that companies don't have lairloads of cash to pay for frivolity anymore. Too bad. It was a good run.

Like I said, it just slipped my mind that I still had the lair down there. Also, I thought that the six deadbolts on the door leading to "the basement" or "John's Workshop" (see how easy that was?) were securely bolted to prevent any unauthorized entrance. Boy is my face red.

Again, kudos to you for getting past all the booby traps. Surviving that one with all the butcher knives that spring from the ceiling is quite a feat. I tested the bejesus out of that one on a number of taller stray dogs and felt sure that it would work. But, like my father always told me, "Taller stray dogs are not humans, John." My dad. Most of his advice sucked, but this piece of advice was gold.

Regarding the pinky toe that you found near one of the sunken pits—I hold steadfast in my argument that it was a potato chip. Sure, I cannot be ABSOLUTELY sure that it was not a toe. But odds are that it was one of those thicker kettle cooked potato chips. A thicker potato chip with a toenail stuck on it makes more sense than a pinky toe, doesn't it?

In the end, what this tells me is that either I need to ratchet up security OR that you are a fabulously intelligent and beautiful woman. Which is it, I ask myself?

Let's be honest, girl, it's probably a little bit of both.

JAVIER

ILLUSTRATED BY SANDRA DIECKMANN

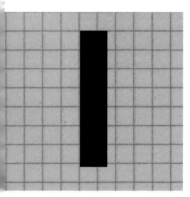 found a baby wolf in the woods and I trained him with honey mustard pretzels to do my bidding.

I named him Javier. He was grey colored, but once I dyed his fur green for a St. Patrick's Day parade. Some people will say that you cannot take the wild out of a wolf, but we all know that you can take the wild out of anything with enough honey mustard flavored snacks.

Like most wolf owners, I shampooed Javier with coconut-scented shampoo and dressed him in a very stylish dog tuxedo. I brought him everywhere with me—to the bar, to the park where I played Frisbee golf, to the barbershop where I drank when the bar hadn't opened yet. Wherever we went, people wouldn't stop with the questions.

"What kind of dog is that?" they asked.

"He's a German Shepherd mix," I said.

"He looks like a very dapper and sophisticated wolf," they told me.

"He gets that a lot," I told them.

After I'd had Javier for a while, my neighbor Angie rescued a bobcat or a lynx from a dumpster down by the Hardee's. She named him Milo and nursed him back to health with Hot Cheetos. Neither of us was sure if Milo was a bobcat or a lynx, but if anyone asked, Angie told them that Milo was just a regular old cat with a very bad gland problem.

I'd had a crush on Angie for a long time, but she still was with her stupid boyfriend Jake. Jake was a poker player, but he wasn't any good. Sometimes when Javier and I crouched underneath their kitchen window we listened to them fight about how much money Jake had lost that week.

"Why does she stay with him?" I asked Javier. "Wouldn't she be happier with me?"

Most nights I sat in my easy chair and Javier curled up near my feet and I explained to him how great it would be to have Angie as my girlfriend, how pretty she was and how desperately I wanted to kiss each one of the ten or so freckles she had running across the bridge of her nose. We also talked about how cool it would be for Javier to hang out with Milo. Both Javier and I thought that lynx or bobcat was pretty fucking chill.

Over the next few weeks, I talked more and more about Angie with Javier. I was really obsessed with her and the life we might have if she would just break up with Jake. Javier was getting tired of hearing about this. When I would start in, he would start to whine and use his paws to cover up his ears.

One afternoon, I saw Jake out sitting on the hood of his car talking on his cell phone and I couldn't help mentioning Jake's stupidity and my undying love for Angie to Javier again. Javier stared up at me and then he sighed deeply. In a few minutes he got up and he slid out his wolf door. About ten minutes later he came back inside and dropped Jake's bloody head right at my feet.

At least, I assumed it was Jake's head. It was pretty hard to tell with all that blood and the fang and claw marks across his face and neck.

"This is Jake's head, right?" I asked Javier.

Javier barked once, which meant yes.

"Wow," I said. "Did you do this for me?"

Javier barked one time again and I grabbed his body and we rolled around on the floor, giggling.

The next morning I knocked on Angie's door. When she answered, I could tell she had been crying. She told me that Jake was dead.

"I always knew it was only a matter of time before he pissed off some loan shark or mob boss," she told me. "I thought they might cut off his hand first, not his head."

Angie sat down on her couch and I sat down next to her and put my arm around her to comfort her.

"Maybe this is for the best," I told her.

From where we sat, we could see her backyard. We could see Milo and Javier playing together out there, chasing a tennis ball around in the grass. I squeezed Angie tighter and she laid her head very gently on my chest.

"Maybe it is," she said.

I ONLY HAVE SEX WITH LADIES NAMED JEAN

ILLUSTRATED BY BILL FERENC

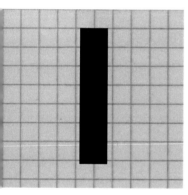

only have sex with ladies named Jean because my name is Gene and because while I certainly love to hear my name being yelled out during sex, I also think it is dope to call out my own name while I fuck.

Gene, Gene, Gene, oh, oh, oh, I usually yell. Yesterday I yelled too loud and my mom came down to the basement and found me with Jean from her bridge club in my bed. I slammed my door and screamed, "Go away! I demand privacy! I occasionally pay rent here!" Finally my mom went back upstairs and I apologized profusely to Jean by fucking her on top of our washing machine.

Sadly there aren't many women named Jean left in my town who have hips that move very well, so I'm thinking about maybe moving to a larger city where most of the Jeans aren't seventy-year-olds with asses that feel like wet bread.

This afternoon, I find my mom scrubbing cherry lube off the washing machine and I tell her about my new plan.

"Great," she says, "I'll start packing your bags."

These are the kinds of things that my mother's been saying to me for a few years now. I usually don't listen, but this time it really got me thinking. Lately I've noticed she's repeating herself a ton—move out, I'll pack your bags, you need to leave here now, etc., etc. I'm not a doctor, but uh-oh, huh? I mean, wouldn't it totally make sense that all this anger and resentment toward me is actually Alzheimer's? It would make a lot of sense to me.

Anyway, I guess I'll keep a closer eye on her now. Because of this new diagnosis and because of my easy access to a washing machine for clean clothes and laundry room sex, I'll probably stick it out here at home for a little while longer. Maybe I'll find some younger Jeans on the Internet or something. Or maybe I'll just change my name to Summer or Crystal so I'll still be able to yell out my name and also do it with some totally hot skanks.

THE FUTURE

ILLUSTRATED BY AMTK

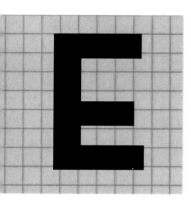

Every September, my uncle Fergus knocked out the donkey with his wooden board and then took him to the vet to get his shots.

"Why don't you just walk him there? Or have the vet drive out?" I asked. "That's how it is done nowadays."

"And yet," Uncle Fergus told me, "that is NOT how our family does things."

Uncle Fergus hooked his thumbs under the straps of his overalls and turned toward the mountains, which meant he was done discussing this with me.

One September, Uncle Fergus had trouble knocking the donkey out. He'd grown weak, and when he smacked the donkey on the head, the donkey just stood there, unfazed.

"John," Uncle Fergus said to me, "I need your help."

I had already decided that things weren't going to be like this when the farm passed onto me. I had talked to some developers by then, had big plans to turn all this land into a huge theme park with roller coasters and frozen banana stands and jolly robot bears that played banjos and sang popular music. All that would have to wait now, though.

"All right," I told him. "Just this once."

Uncle Fergus looked distraught when he passed his wooden donkey knocking out board to me. His eyes welled up. I think he understood that he would never have the strength to swing that board again. I turned toward that donkey. He was none too pleased either, his one good eye staring up at me.

"Okay," Uncle Fergus said. "Go on, then."

I gripped the board in my hands. I'll admit it felt really good. I knew it had been passed down from generation to generation, this finely lacquered piece of hard donkey knocking out oak. I stepped back and took a couple of warm up swings.

"I'm ready now," I told my uncle.

I planted my feet firmly on the ground and wound up and swung at the donkey's head. I was about to smack the beast and be done with all of this, but at the last second my uncle slid right in front of me. I tried to stop my momentum, but there was just no way. I hit Uncle Fergus square on the temple and he grunted once and then he fell over, dead.

ILLUSTRATED BY LAURA ANDREWS

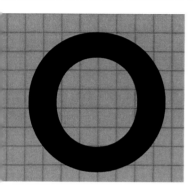

kay James, you're my charming older brother, so I took the time out of my lunch hour at PetSmart to drive over here and speak to you in person about this incident that occurred yesterday afternoon. As I told you on the phone, I can certainly understand your need to find the person (or persons) responsible for this brilliantly calculated act of glorious vengeance. Just know going in that I expect to be fully reimbursed for mileage.

First of all, bro, let me just say that I am absolutely stunned by this series of events. Totally shocked and appalled! I know that from speaking to Jules, your achingly hot trophy wife, that she thinks this was an inside job, some petty jealousy that boiled over into this brilliantly passive-aggressive act of sweet malice. And since she is so hot, she is certainly entitled to that misguided opinion. But the fact remains that this crime has all the hallmarks of a devious European criminal mastermind. I suspect that this person (or persons) we are dealing with probably has a dashing nickname. Something like "The Mamba" or maybe "Scorpio." Or maybe, he or she is a person who is smart enough to reserve the right to use a more dashing nickname when he or she thinks of it.

In my experience, you just don't catch someone like "The Mantis" (is that better?), unless of course, they want to be caught. He or she is probably already way out of the country now, blissfully tucked away on a tropical island enjoying a piña colada. For instance, if I close my eyes right now I can imagine "The Mantis" riding on a jet ski, a beautiful brunette that looks very similar to Jules wrapped around his waist. Ah, "The Mantis." I will open my eyes right now before I fall too deeply in love with him, all right?

Anyway James, from talking to our mother, I already know you have been hard at work trying to discern the secret identity of the villain (or group of villains) who committed this heinous act. I know that you've been working the phones all morning, feverishly dialing up everyone on your guest list and asking if anyone at your birthday party had seen anything untoward happening to your dishwasher. Do you honestly think that a criminal mastermind like the "The Falconer"—that is probably a cooler name isn't it?—would have slipped up so easily and been seen by any of your party guests? It is not very likely when he or she had probably planned this devious act to the most minute detail since your last birthday.

Deep within my bosom, James, I can't help feeling that this is partly my fault. I am your brother, related by blood and other genetic fluids, and I should have kept a much closer eye on your dishwasher. I should have never let some interloper sneak a Ziploc freezer bag packed to the brim with feces into your house disguised as a birthday present. I also should never have let this person disappear at the precise moment when everyone was busy watching you blow out your birthday candles. I mean, honestly, you can't even possibly understand just how much I am probably beating myself up over this. At least we have one clue though, right? We know that "The Falconer" certainly likes corn.

So reality check, James: not all is lost. I think we can come out of this with some lessons learned, right? Here's one: when you match wits with "The Lamprey" (there we go, that sounds right, "The Lamprey!"), your life ends up in total shambles. First, you have to replace your brand new dishwasher. Then in a couple of months your hot wife will probably leave you for this mysterious and cunning evil super-genius, "The Lamprey."

Whoever he may be.

THE BEAR

ILLUSTRATED BY JENNIFER DAVIS

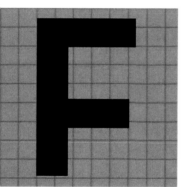

or starters, the bear was going to stop eating out of the White Castle dumpster. Next, he was going to stop drinking gin. Lastly, no more sex outside his species.

This morning he'd woken up with his eyebrows gone and the words "Wolf Fucker" written in permanent marker on his forehead. The last thing he remembered was standing in front of a microphone and singing the song "Hello" by Lionel Richie.

"Why do I keep doing these things?" he asked himself. "I'm supposed to be smarter than this."

The bear slept for a bit in the sun and when he woke he had a blinding headache. He grabbed a salmon out of the river, shoved it into his mouth, and chewed.

He walked downstream. While he walked he caught a reflection of his face in the river. The missing eyebrows did not look all that bad. In fact, he thought his face now looked younger, more upbeat.

Later that day, he got a text from his Russian friend, Gregor, who he hadn't talked to since they'd eaten that park ranger, badge and all.

"Wanna party?" Gregor asked.

The bear was feeling better now. And he was already sick of fighting these awful urges, to drink and to fuck pretty wolves. He grabbed a squirrel by the tail and threw it against a tree.

"Let's do this shit!" he texted back.

A TOAST TO RANDY,
THE OLDEST SON OF MY SECRET
FAMILY

ILLUSTRATED BY MEGHAN MURPHY SUSZYNSKI

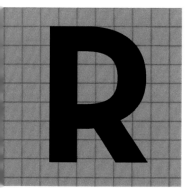

andy, we have gathered here in Cleveland to celebrate you and your new bride, Chelsea's, entrance into this blessed union. I know I've missed a lot of your formative years on the road as an industrial cleaning supplies salesman, but son, there was no way that I was going to miss this. Even with all that godforsaken road construction on I-80, I just had to come.

Last night, when I was driving here from Des Moines, on what my other family thinks is yet another "unavoidable sales call," it brought me back to that day when you were born. So long ago. I know I've told you that story a thousand times, but I thought I would share it with everyone here tonight.

Back in the days before cell phones, it was so much more difficult to have a secret family. I see some of the men in the crowd nodding. Am I right, guys, or am I right? Nowadays, any doofus with a calling plan can have a secret family. Randy, look at your half-wit uncle, David—even HE can handle a secret family. He can hardly cut his meat by himself, but he's got over nine children in three different states and two in one U.S. Commonwealth, and all of them think they are part of his "real" family. Kudos to him. Back when you were born, Randy, wow—you really had to be on your toes when you were forced to use landlines.

For instance, that magical day you were born. I walked down to Manny's Good Time—this bar down the street from my other house—and pretended that I was calling your mother from a hotel room. It worked, but let me tell you, it is damn hard to shush a room full of union electricians hopped up on Old Crow. Everyone was still getting used to this idea of a secret family; they were not nearly as sympathetic as they are today. Today you walk in anywhere and hold up the international sign for "I'm placing a call to my secret family" and everyone shuts the hell up. People then were just not as understanding. We really owe a lot to Steve Garvey for that; we really, really do.

Anyway, when your mother told me about you, Randy, I could hardly contain myself. I remember I was so excited that I walked back home to my other family and ate a turkey sandwich. Then, I read my other kids a bedtime story and then kissed them goodnight. Then I screwed my other wife. What a night! I was so proud. And when I finally got to hold you on my sales route two weeks later—you know how everyone says that nothing can compare to the first time you hold your secret baby—well, Randy, I couldn't agree more.

I give you this advice, my son, because someday soon you'll be driving down some road somewhere and you'll suddenly realize that one family is definitely not enough for you. You'll suddenly realize that you are only spending fifty percent of your familial energy and that you have at least 75-80 percent more to give. Where will it be? Detroit? Boise? Clay Center, Nebraska? What I am trying to say is that if I hadn't pulled over when I had that feeling, if I wouldn't have stopped at that diner that your mother worked at, if I hadn't told your mother that I was allergic to latex and that I couldn't wear a condom without getting an awful rash, if I hadn't pretended that your mother was the only woman in my life and that I loved her and her alone, none of this would have happened. No you, no wedding, no toast. None of us would be enjoying these lovely pork medallions right now.

Now, a secret family isn't to be entered into lightly. You've got to really make a commitment. Sure, sure, you're saying, I hear you dad, I hear you, I am a smart guy, I know what I'm getting into here. But there's a lot of talk in the news lately about these absentee secret fathers, men who didn't listen to the advice from their elders, men who thought they could figure it out by them-selves. Don't let that happen to you, son. You are the future; don't become another statistic.

Okay, I see I am getting the international sign to wrap it up here from your mom, so I will. It's okay, I've had my say, and honestly, I've got a phone call to make back to Des Moines where I have to pretend I am not drunk. My youngest, Travis, had an AAU soccer game tonight that I missed to come here. Let's just hope that the game went as well for him as this night is going for Randy and Chelsea! What a great night! Anyway, can I thank everyone here in advance for keeping it down for a couple of minutes while I make that call to Des Moines? Thanks then, thanks in advance.

So yes, everyone, raise your glasses, a toast to the lovely couple, Randy and Chelsea! May they stride forth with long intrepid steps and give my secret wife and me many secret grandchildren to love and spoil. Salud!

the pretty thing puts the lotion in the basket

THE LADY AT THE TEMP AGENCY SAID I WASN'T SUPPOSED TO LET YOU GUYS OUT OF YOUR CAGES

ILLUSTRATED BY RACHEL CALDWELL

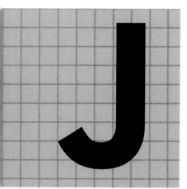

Jesus, what is it now, guys? This is the second time I've had to come down here in the last ten days and I can't say that I am very pleased. I was busy upstairs doing my Sudoku and I had to put that aside and tromp down here to listen to your bellyaching. You're hungry, you're tired, you're caged in 3' × 5' steel boxes. On and on. Next time I walk down those stairs somebody better have fucking died. And for the last time, Jim doesn't count. Jim was dead when I was down here last week.

So good try, but I'm going back upstairs. The lady at the temp agency said you would try to trick me like this, beg me to give you more to eat than your mini box of Wheaties and your weekly ration of water. She said that you'd try to be funny, too—saying things like "the pretty thing puts the lotion in the basket"—but she warned me that every word out of your mouths was just a ruse to get me to open your cages. Let me tell you right now: that isn't going to happen. Even though I really can't remember what her name is—Janice? Jennine? Audrey?—that lady at the temp agency really stuck her neck out to get me this job. I'll be damned if I disappoint her now.

I know, I know, when I was drunk last week I came down here and regaled you with rousing tales of my previous workplace indiscretions—how I stole all those AA batteries and Post-it notes from my previous employer's supply cabinet, how I took a piss in that ficus, how all those girls from all those jobs filed all those restraining orders—I am sure telling you all those stick-it-to-the-man tales gave you hope that I would be lax in my duties here. That is what you thought, right?

What you need to understand is that I am just like any other guy who works for seven dollars an hour with no health or dental benefits—I take pride in a job well done. Now, I'm not saying that I'm perfect. I still occasionally dip into the supply cabinet to steal some pens and pencils for home use. But I'm improving, okay? For example, I hardly ever revenge piss anymore.

Yes, the lady at the temp agency said you guys were going to be tricky. Especially the cute one, she said. The cute one is their leader, she told me, watch the cute one. Actually, since all of you are rail thin and your teeth are getting kind of mossy, I can't really be sure who the cute one is anymore. No offense, but if we had a beauty contest right now, I'm not sure I wouldn't vote for Jim over the rest of you. Even though his nose was chewed off by those rats, he still has this quiet dignity about him that I think is really amazing.

Anyway, back to the grind, guys. Just so you know, I have a colleague named Lauren coming over here later tonight for a business meeting. Even though Lauren usually drinks enough to black out, I would really appreciate if you kept your moaning and your clinking of your metal cups on your cages to a bare minimum. Please remember that some of us are trying to work around here.

special

Spicy

24 hrs

EAT

HOT

sweet

CHEAP

BEEF

CHILI!

TASTY

OPEN

NIGHTLY

SAUSAGE

THE HOOKERS IN MY NEIGHBORHOOD REALLY LOVE MY CHILI

ILLUSTRATED BY ANNE ULKU

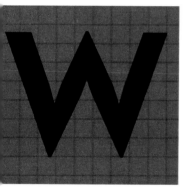

hen I drink, I smoke. When I drink AND smoke, sometimes I light cars on fire. If it's a Wednesday night, I get out my fog machine and invite some friends over to dance. This is a pretty understanding neighborhood unless you wear assless chaps after Labor Day.

Once at one of my dance parties, a hooker told me I made good chili and asked me for my recipe. I traded it to her for sex on my porch swing. You may think this is an amazing turn of events, but this wasn't even the first time that had happened. Hookers love my chili so much that they usually thank me for it with sex on my kitchen floor or in my broom closet.

The other day I was drunk and smoking and I left the bar and went and lit a Subaru hatchback on fire. As I was walking away, I realized there were two people making out in the backseat of the car and so I ran back and got them out before the car exploded.

"You were pretty lucky I was around to save your life," I told the couple. They nodded yes and then began to show me their thanks by taking off their pants and making out with me. As you can probably guess by now, this wasn't the first time this kind of thing has happened to me, but it was definitely some of the best non-hooker thank you sex in my recent memory.

Some people in this neighborhood will probably tell you that I am not the best neighbor, but honestly, they don't know how hard I work at being selfless. For instance, yesterday I made a double batch of chili and then drove over to the street where the hookers work. I brought my fog machine and I created a huge wall of fog and then I jumped through the fog wall and yelled, "Surprise! Chili!" This was obviously a big hit among all my hooker friends. They all screamed "Hooray!" and then we rented a suite in a hotel and screwed and ate lunch.

SORRY, BUT I JUST CAN'T MARRY A WOMAN THAT DOESN'T LOOK HOT ON THE JUMBOTRON

ILLUSTRATED BY KYLE COUGHLIN

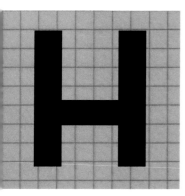

ey Sarah, remember how ten seconds ago I was just down on one knee and I gave you that ring and everyone in the stadium cheered for us? Well, I'd like to take it back now. The ring, the proposal, everything. I know, I know, you are still jumping around and you've just called your parents and everyone in our section is backslapping and handshaking, but I just don't think this is going to work out for me now.

Why, you ask? Well, to tell you the truth, I just finished watching the replay of my proposal in high resolution and I've got to tell you that I realized I made a Jumbotron-sized mistake. Look here, there's the replay of the proposal up there on the screen again. Now watch closely—see right there, when I snap open the ring box and I look up into your eyes and ask for your hand in marriage—I look really good, right? My t-shirt accentuates my pecs and I am exuding a confident, yet somewhat shy air.

Now look at you, right there—Jesus. See how your face pinches up when I pop the question? In real life, you are a scorchingly hot woman, but on the Jumbotron, where it counts, your beauty just wilts away. I don't even know what to say. Honestly, look at that, right when you say yes to me. I can hardly even recognize you. You look jowly, a little jaundiced, and vaguely masculine. Like Andie McDowell after a fistfight and too many whippets.

Don't fret, darling. This is one of life's great mysteries—why some people look hot in real life and some people look hot in real life AND on the Jumbotron. I don't know if any scientists have studied this, but I would be willing to argue that some people just lose something in the translation of their flesh into pixels. Maybe it has to do with the fact that when you are enlarged to fifty square feet, your true beauty is more readily evident to the naked eye. That's just one man's take.

Anyway, what this boils down to, Sarah, is that I can't marry you. I'm sorry, but as a season ticket holder to a number of major sporting events, I can't be with a girl who doesn't make everyone absolutely drool when she is put on the kissing cam or randomly shown doing the wave or yelling "Charge!" Call me a purist, but that's just the way it is.

So it's back to the single life for me, I guess. I know it is going to be an arduous battle to find my special new lady, but I'll keep searching because I know she's out there somewhere.

I AM SO SORRY THAT MY HOMING DEVICE
WAS CHAFING YOUR ANKLE

ILLUSTRATED BY TUESDAY BASSEN

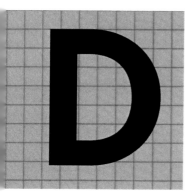

earest Josie,

Given the perspective that thirty-eight minutes apart usually gives, I think we can agree that this homing device business was a big mistake. I don't know for sure if it was the biggest mistake I ever made in our relationship—just another one that gave you a hellish rash.

So come back home, baby, come back right now. I can tell you that things have already changed for the better. I mean, if you saw me now, compared to the person I was those thirty-eight long minutes ago, I bet you'd even hardly recognize me. Really. I had an epiphany. Three of them. Back to back to back. I put on cologne and I smell way less like Slim Jims now. Totally new man. Wow.

For one, I've had time to really rethink things. I sketched out some schematics for a new homing device that I'd love to show you, but try these improvements on for size—no more exposed gears, lower levels of lead poisoning, and a quieter beeping sound coming from your pants. Too good to be true, right? Well, as an added bonus, I also promise that I won't be swayed by that hot salesgirl at Home Depot to go with the cut-rate brushed aluminum when what a woman like you really deserves is gold (plating).

Number two realization—yes, okay, I admit it, I smothered you. Wanting to know where you were AT ALL TIMES was probably somewhat intrusive. From now on, you can just tell me where you are going to be (let's work out the exact schedule later, but I was thinking something like Tuesday mornings from 5:30 a.m.–6:00 a.m.), and I'll just trust you. That will be one of the new rules. I don't have any other new rules yet, but I think that this one really speaks to the kind of guy I've become in the last thirty-eight minutes—conscientious, able to control my emotions, even keel. The old me needed to know where you were at 24–7–365, but the new me only needs to know, longitudinally and latitudinally down to the millimeter, exactly where you are for the other 167 hours and 30 minutes of each week.

Jo-Jo baby, I understand when you come back if you might want to take it slow. Totally understandable. I am waiting here for you whenever you choose to come home from wherever it is you are (looks like you are just crossing into Kansas). I mean, I can come find you if I need to (just outside Topeka is what my computer is saying), but I can certainly give you some space (I'll be on the road in about five minutes time if I don't see your car turn around) and see what happens.

So come back home. I love you. We'll just file this in our "learning experience" folder and go out to eat at El Toritos. While we are there, I'll tell you how sexy your new gold (plated) homing device looks and how I can hardly even hear it beeping over the courageous ballads of their eighteen-piece mariachi band.

Soon,

Todd

MY CODPIECE SMELLS LIKE SOUP

ILLUSTRATED BY TERRENCE PAYNE

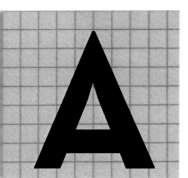

A few days ago, I was in my backyard rehearsing a play I'd written about my ex-girlfriend, Daphne. I was wearing a codpiece and swinging around a bullwhip because there was a lot of codpiece-wearing and bullwhipping in the script. I'd written a number of plays about Daphne in the last few months, but in my humble opinion this one was the best.

While I rehearsed, my neighbor Theo popped his head over my fence and asked me if he could borrow my codpiece. Theo was a playwright too. There are a lot of playwrights in my neighborhood and sometimes codpieces and fog machines are very hard to come by.

"Is it going to come back smelling like soup?" I asked.

I asked Theo this because once I'd lent him my hacksaw and it came back smelling like soup. It was hard to believe, but I kept putting my nose up to the saw blade and there was no escaping it—beef fucking barley.

"What the hell are you talking about?" Theo asked.

Listen—I knew I did not have to do this favor for Theo. He was not my boss and I was taller than him if I wore my tall shoes. Still, I needed to regain some goodwill from my neighbors. There had been an incident a few weeks ago where I'd borrowed my neighbor Gary's theremin, and Daphne and I ended up having sex in front of it and her moans and my moans and the moans of the theremin mixed together into one very loud moan. Everyone on my block heard this moaning because it was the night of our neighborhood block party for which we'd signed up to bring strawberry cheesecake but hadn't brought any strawberry cheesecake.

"It's hard to find a good codpiece," I told Theo as I set the codpiece into his open palm. "It's damn hard to find a codpiece that strikes a happy balance of fit and comfort and shows off your junk in the proper way."

I thought I'd impressed upon Theo the importance of returning my codpiece exactly as I'd given it to him, but when he brought it back the next day, it smelled like soup again. This time it smelled like broccoli and fucking cheddar.

"Not cool," I told him. "Really not cool."

"What's not cool?" he said.

That night, I scrubbed my codpiece but I couldn't get rid of the soup smell. I went to bed angry, but when I awoke the sun was out and I was feeling better. I decided then and there that living well would be the best revenge for Theo and the rest of them, so I went back out to my backyard and rehearsed my play some more. There's a rusted out school bus sitting next to my house that I've been meaning to fix up for about the last ten years and I snapped my bullwhip at it over and over until I felt like myself again.

GET IN
IF YOU WANT TO LIVE

ILLUSTRATED BY MATTHEW RONES

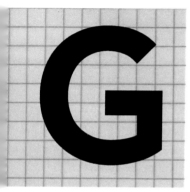

et in if you want to live. That's what the dude in the truck that looked like a tank said to me. I hate that pickup line. Yes, there were fireballs raining from the sky and sure, I could hear that roving band of zombies moaning in the distance, but "get in if you want to live"? Really? I get that line like twenty times a day now. If you are trying to hook up with this sweet piece of post-apocalyptic ass, you're gonna need to try way harder than that, mister.

It's not like I'm even picky anymore, all right? This guy wasn't really my type—he had a bunch of matted blood and trail mix in his beard and his eyes were all kinds of rapey—still, if he would have gone with something timeless like, "Hi, what's your name?" I probably would have hopped in with him in a second. I tend to give non-zombies with tank-trucks a lot of latitude, and with a couple of reasonable words and a smile with more than two or three viable teeth, I usually say let's give our love a shot.

What I said instead was, no, no, I'm fine, I'll just keep enjoying my walk along this beautiful piece of charred earth in my shoes that are made of duct tape, breathing this air that smells like leather, and getting ready to eat my last can of pumpkin pie filling, thank you very much.

After I told him this, the man shook his head and yelled, "It's your funeral, lady!" Then he peeled out. It's your funeral? What the fuck? Sometimes I just get so sick of all these unoriginal men saying all these absolutely predictable things that I just want to throw something at them. Luckily in this case, there was a detached arm sitting on the ground near me and I picked it up and chucked it at him. Lately, I've become quite adept at throwing detached arms and legs, so I was not surprised to see the arm land on the roof of his truck with a loud smack. I figured this guy would just keep on driving, but then I saw brake lights. And then I heard that telltale beep-beep-beep backing up truck-tank sound. And then I did what I always do when this happens—I started running toward the gutted out Applebee's that I call home.

I didn't quite make it there. This guy's truck was fast and my legs were weak from only eating pie filling for the last month. When he caught up to me, he jumped out of his truck and said, "Lady, I'm your worst nightmare."

I mean, of course he did, because what else would a dope like this say in that situation? He was coming toward me with a knife and I blocked a couple of his wild swings with my can of pie filling. And then I turned the can on him. I smacked him with it in the temple once and then I jumped on top of him. I began to hit him in the head over and over until the can broke open and there was this big mess of pumpkin and brain everywhere. Unfortunately, in the process, I ruined my favorite pair of duct tape slacks.

After I brushed myself off, I saw the tank truck sitting there and I thought to myself: why shouldn't I live a little? The keys were in the ignition and in the glove compartment there was a Led Zeppelin CD. I started up the truck and put in the CD and then I flew off down the road, listening to Robert Plant scream "AHHHIIIAAAHHHAAA!" again and again. Whenever I saw a zombie I drove straight into them and laughed as I watched their bodies totally fucking explode.

ILLUSTRATED BY ANDY DUCETT

y best friend Joe looks like Handel and I look like Beethoven. Ladies always ask us if we are them and we tell them hell yes. Man, do we. It is all about the ladies.

Tonight, Joe and I got invited to a hot tub party.

Do Beethoven, the partiers said, do Handel.

I sat in the hot water and pretended I was Beethoven. I moved my long hair out of my face and any time someone asked me something I said "What?" and pointed to my ears.

One of the partiers was a blonde lady named Suzy. She tried to flirt with me by humming "Ode to Joy," but she'd taken too many Quaaludes from the Quaaludes bowl to really remember how it went.

"I know I'm supposed to already be deaf, but can you shut the hell up anyway?" I asked.

Just like Beethoven, I don't like blondes.

Joe has a bad drinking problem. When I drink, I steal.

We are not the best party guests, but we are not the worst either. We always bring a bottle of red wine and if the fancy grocery store is open we bring the footiest smelling cheese they have.

"Is he dead?" one of the people at the party asked me after Joe passed out. "Did Handel just die in the hot tub?"

Sometimes when Joe passes out he looks like he's totally dead, but then he will suddenly wake up and punch his hand through a bathroom door or a bay window. He never remembers any of it.

Tonight I'd stolen three wallets and a purse by the time Joe kicked a hole in the hot tub. I was making out with this brunette named Jessica near the pool and I noticed bubbling water spilling out around my legs.

"Uh-oh." Jessica pointed. "Here comes Tony."

I saw a huge, shirtless man moving toward me. I got up to run, but it was too late. Tony grabbed me by the throat and lifted me off the ground.

"You and your friend have ten seconds to get your classical asses out of here," he said.

After Joe and I get kicked out of parties, we like to go downtown and sit in the park by the river. It used to be a bad part of town, but then the mayor decided to pipe in classical music. Now the drug dealers have moved on and the hookers are higher class. Tonight, I buy us burgers and fries and slap Joe around until he can hold a decent conversation.

"I am sorry about before," he tells me. "I am sorry about always."

I stare out at the river water, the lights of the city skyline bleeding downstream in the current.

"There will be other parties," I tell Joe. "And other ladies."

This is what I always tell Joe when we get kicked out of parties, but lately I'm starting to not believe it. There is a crash of cymbals and a swell of strings above our heads and I wonder how much longer we will look this fucking beautiful.

THE
END

JOHN JODZIO

I FINALLY HAVE MY BODY DISMORPHIA UNDER CONTROL.

is a winner of the Loft-McKnight Fellowship and the author of the short story collection, *If You Lived Here You'd Already Be Home* (Replacement Press, 2010). His stories have appeared in McSweeney's, One Story, Barrelhouse, Opium, The Florida Review, and various other places in print and online. He lives in Minneapolis with his wife and son and dominates in both frisbee and regular golf.

SELF-PORTRAIT BY JOHN JODZIO

PHOTO BY LOUISA PODLICH

GET IN IF YOU WANT TO **LIVE**

MISSY AUSTIN is originally from Cedarburg, Wisconsin, and received her BA from the University of Minnesota. She lives and works in Minneapolis as a Junior Art Director at Zeus Jones ad agency.

ROBERT JAMES ALGEO is a Philadelphian illustrator, cartoonist, and educator currently living in Minneapolis. He received his MFA in Comic Art from the Minneapolis College of Art and Design in 2011.

ANDRES GUZMAN was born in Lima, Peru, and spent most of his life in Denver, Colorado, before moving to Minnesota to attend the Minneapolis College of Art and Design. He graduated from MCAD in 2009 and has been featured in *Wired*, *CMYK*, and *FRONT Magazine*.

CARLEYRAE WEBER was born and raised in Sturgeon Bay, Wisconsin, but made her home in Macerata, Italy after graduating from the Milwaukee Institute of Art and Design in 2007. Her work has been purchased for private and public collections around the world.

RUBEN IRELAND is a graphic artist and illustrator based in London. His clients include Urban Outfitters, Society6, and *Junkfood Magazine*. He works in a variety of mediums including handmade textures, ink drawings, and digital collage.

MEGAN FRAUENHOFFER was born in St. Louis, Missouri, and received her MFA in Printmaking from the Minneapolis College of Art and Design in 2010. Her work has been featured in *Beautiful/Decay Book: 6* and *FIND Art Magazine*.

AINARA DEL VALLE was born in Spain and attended college for engineering before switching her focus to art. She attended the Miami Ad School for Art Direction and has worked for top agencies in London, Stockholm, and Germany.

JENNIFER DAVIS is a Minneapolis artist to the core. Born and raised in Minnesota, Davis received her BFA in Painting and Drawing from the University of Minnesota in 1998 and has been supporting herself with her art since 2003.

SANDRA DIECKMANN is a native of Germany currently residing in East London. She received her first class honours BA degree in Graphic Information Design at the University of Westminster in London. Her work has been featured in *AMMO Magazine*, *Juxtapoz Magazine*, and *Creaturemag*.

MEGHAN MUPRHY is the Creative Director for Paper Darts. She received a BA in Art, English, and Art History from the University of Minnesota. She works as a freelance graphic designer from her tiny desk in uptown Minneapolis under the name Cloud Carvings.

BILL FERENC was born and raised in the lovely little town of Wyandotte, Michigan. He lives and works in Minneapolis where he received his BA from the Minneapolis College of Art and Design. Past clients include Spunk Design Machine, Fallon Worldwide, and Target.

RACHEL CALDWELL is an illustrator and designer based in Philadelphia, Pennsylvania, where she received her BFA from Kutztown University. Her freelance clients include Urban Outfitters, Threadless, Society6, and Fender Musical Instruments.

AMTK is the creative brainchild of Minneapolis artists Andie Mazorol and Tynan Kerr. The pair work in tandem on both the conception and completion of their oil paintings.

ANNE ULKU graduated from the Minneapolis College of Art and Design in 2007 and works fulltime as a freelance typographer and illustrator. She is the brains behind ongoing design projects Six Word Story Every Day and DailyHues.

LAURA ANDREWS works and lives in Minneapolis. She teaches painting and drawing at Minneapolis Community and Technical College and at Century College in White Bear Lake.

KYLE COUGHLIN is the Assistant Creative Director for Paper Darts. He works as a freelance graphic designer and illustrator from his home in Minneapolis. He received his BA in Graphic Design from the Art Institute of Phoenix in 2007.

 **TUESDAY BASSEN** is an illustrator currently residing in New York City. She received her MFA from the Minneapolis College of Art and Design is one half of the design blog Studio-Sweet-Studio, which features the work and workspaces of artists.

 **MATTHEW KUNES** received his BA in Graphic Design and Printmaking from the University of Wisconsin—Stout. He lives in Minneapolis and is the owner of Motelprint Studios.

 **TERRENCE PAYNE** has been filling Minneapolis with amazing art for over fifteen years. He is the founder and gallery director of Rosalux Gallery in Northeast Minneapolis, where he has helped hundreds of artists share and develop their work.

 **ANDY DUCETT** received his MFA from the University of Illinois and his BFA from the University of Wisconsin—Stout. He teaches at the College of Visual Arts in Saint Paul, the Minneapolis College of Art and Design, and the University of Wisconsin—Stout.

Paper Darts Press represents a new approach to creative publishing based on the intimate collaboration between an author, artist, and publisher trifecta. Through unconventional printing practices, beautiful design, and a uniting underdog attitude, Paper Darts Press is leading a Do-It-Yourself and Do-It-Together publishing revolution.

www.paperdarts.org